Back to School Boot Camp
The Crayon Cadet

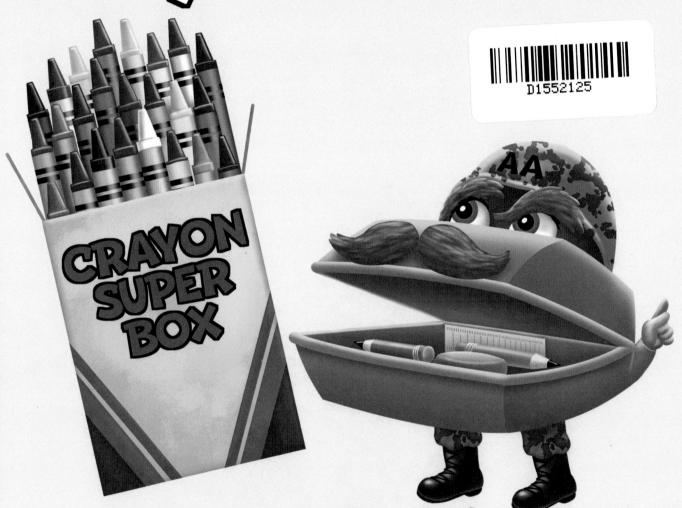

CRAYON SUPER BOX

by Megan Beard and Lisha Hernandez

Illustrations by Mike Motz

To all the teacher besties.
You never know where
you'll find your inspiration!

Back to School Boot Camp
The Crayon Cadet

by Megan Beard and Lisha Hernandez

Illustrations by Mike Motz

Left, left, left, right, left!

Well hello there! It's about that time of year again.
Time for a new set of recruits to join our Academic Army.

I'm Sergeant Ulysses P. Ply, SUPPLY for short.
I've worked many years training
young recruits like yourself.
What are you waiting for?

It's time to get started!

Follow along to learn if you please,
And you can earn badges just like these.
You'll work your way through the ranks you see,

To become a Sergeant just like me!

Your first task as a recruit
is to master the art of crayons.

A Crayon Cadet,
I'll make you one yet!

Open the box and you will see
a rainbow of colors, waiting for you and me.
Each one is ready for a specific job to do,
but it's up to you which one you'll use.

A tree is green, the sky is blue,
a butterfly can be whatever you choose.

Like the world around you, make your art more real,
by choosing the colors from the color wheel.
Red, orange, yellow, purple, green, and blue.
Make all these colors work for you.

A Crayon Cadet sees the picture they get,
And colors to make it the best one yet.

10-HUT!

The color is chosen, and it looks just fine.
It's time for all recruits to fall in line.

As you color, the lines you see
are a guide for where the color should be.
Don't break formation. Stay in the lines.
It's best for our unit if you're neat. Take your time!

Crayon Cadets we all will be,
scribbling and swerving is not the way, you see!

I will show you the way to succeed.
Small strokes and a steady hand are what you will need.
Take your time and do your best.
Let the colorful crayons take care of the rest!

A picture you'll color and artwork you will make,
but there may come a day when your crayon will break.

Never fear, the end isn't near.
A crayon in two is double the gear.
Two pieces of green or two pieces of blue
color just as well as the one that was new.

No matter the damage the wear or tear,
a Crayon Cadet is always fair.
If ever you find yourself in a bind,
remember a Crayon Cadet leaves no crayon behind.

Crayons Fall Out!

When the work is finished
it's time to go home,
no one crayon wants
to be left all alone.

A cadet's job is to make sure
they get put in the right place.
Not shoved in a pocket or stuffed in a space.

They try to roll from the desk to the floor
and can end up in trash cans or roll out of the door.
So as you clean and search the ground,
make sure no crayon is left lying around.

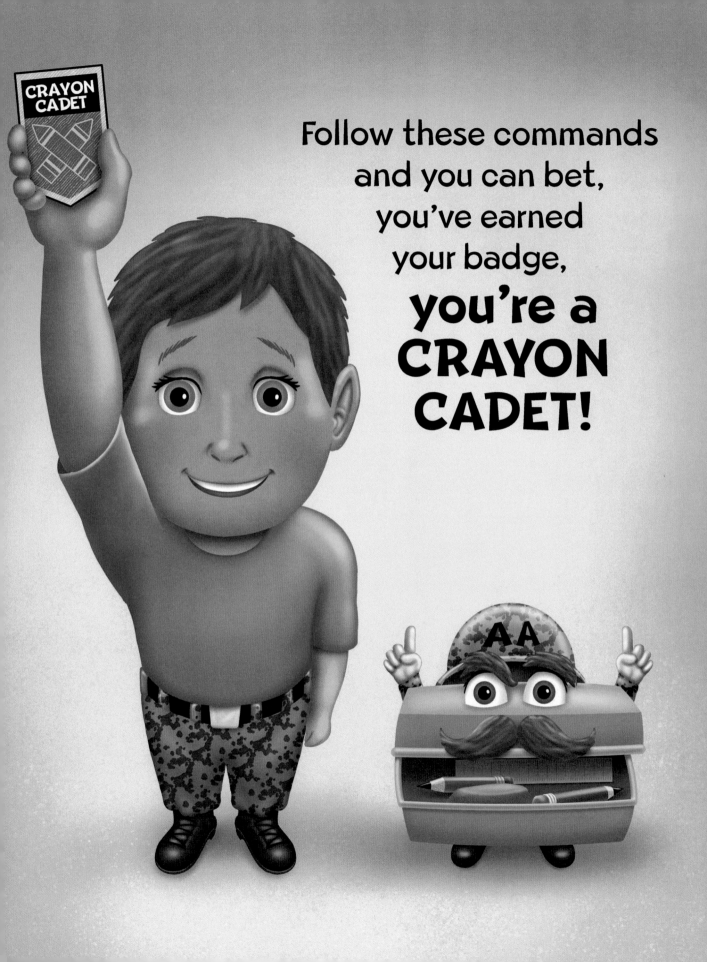

Follow these commands
and you can bet,
you've earned
your badge,
**you're a
CRAYON
CADET!**

Meet Megan Beard and Lisha Hernandez

Megan Beard and Lisha Hernandez are elementary school teachers. They reside and teach in Southeast Texas and met while working on the same campus. It didn't take long for them to become best friends. Together they have a combined experience of over 25 years in teaching. Both having their own kids, and teaching in the classroom has inspired them to write children's books that can be used for a more engaging lesson and to maintain the love of reading in the classroom amongst students and teachers alike.

Made in the USA
Middletown, DE
16 August 2022

71495704R00015